DON'T WAKE ME!

SARAH

God, we keep meeting at the laptop! Thank you. I keep hearing you say: "Keep going, Pooka!" That's all I know to do. I never get tired of writing. I actually enjoy this more than any other gifts I have. It's my passion. When the time is right the world will see what you've been up to in my life. I am grateful you never leave me! Another project and I'm eager to see what you do with this one! My everything, you are!

Churn, thank you for loving me. You don't have a normal mom. That would be boring!!!

I enjoy watching each of you sleep. When you have a bright idea, I'm your biggest cheerleader. When you make a mistake I share with you some of mine. I love when we roast each other. It teaches you that life ain't always serious. Our mini road trips and us acting like we ain't even from VA.

People love to see us being "us!" Our singing in grocery stores. The boy be acting like he "David Ruffin!" (side eye). He get that from his momma. The fact that ya'll so quick to forgive and share your heart and not give a piece of your mind. You have been teaching me that for years. How ya'll continue to cheer for me when I'm tired or can't see the light at the end of any tunnel. How ya'll tell me about the Bible. God is the way....Thank ya'll for being my lil people. I appreciate the way ya'll love me! My

first REAL best friends!!!

Quante Bell

You gotttzzz to be crazy to put up with me…LOL. It's your honesty and the way you deliver it. You're gentle with my heart. Your advice and intuition. You let me be me and don't try to change a thing. Your support whether I am right or wrong, you seldom say: "I told you so." If I mess up you are there to help clean it up. You are very patient with me. Through most of my storms you've held an umbrella and at times have given me your "rain coat." Sir, we've grown through somethings that could have broken us and almost destroyed us. Thank you for loving me and these churn. Being a provider and protector. My best friend. I trust you with me and these churn!!! That means the world to me. Let's continue to be US! I love you!

Synopsis:

Oliver, a deaf mute who solves mysteries in his sleep while dreaming! He's a murder mystery solver. The only way to capture the bad guy is to catch the little boy in a dream state. During therapy he draws what he dreams about; the only problem is the last murder victim was his mother and he hasn't slept good or dreamt much since. They are running out of time and need Oliver to dream so they can

capture the "bad guy!"

I'll always be with you!!

Using hand movements, facial expressions, and sign language Oliver and his mother Sarah were conversing about his therapy session earlier that morning.

"I am glad Ollie. I know some days are better than others. I am glad today was one of them." Sarah said. Sarah and Ollie had just arrived at their house. It was about time for them to enjoy lunch and decide what they were going to eat for dinner. Sarah signed for Ollie to go up to his room and get freshened up while she prepares their lunch. He signed asking her if they could eat and watch the new Avatar movie together in her bedroom. She signed saying yes that would be a great idea. As soon as Ollie reached their staircase leaving their kitchen Sarah's cellphone buzzed. She had received a text message. She looked at her cellphone. Ollie stopped walking up their steps. He felt the vibration and

turned to face his mother. Sarah never

looked up. Her demeanor and facial

expression changed. She felt Ollie

looking at her. She forced a smile on

her face and looked at him. Ollie

signed asking her if everything was ok.

Sarah lied to him and assured him

everything was indeed ok. Ollie knew

better. He felt his mother's energy.

She blew him a kiss and sent him an

air hug. That made him feel better.

He returned the gestures and turned

around to head back upstairs. Sarah's

facial expression changed back to

worrying. With another notification of

a text message coming through she

quickly grabbed her cellphone off the

counter so Ollie couldn't feel the

vibration and turned her back away

from their stairs. She was unsure as to

who the sender was, but she knew

what the messages meant. The texts

read: "I have had more than enough

patience. It hasn't been easy being

away from you all. (She quickly knew

who the sender was.) As soon as this

last drop has been made we will be

together again. Have you done what I

asked of you? Carlos said he hasn't

been able to get in touch with you.

Without you handling your part we

can't be together again. What do you

say? For old time sake? I miss my

family. When this is over and done

with, we can buy that Beachfront Villa

you showed me a picture of in Punta

Cana. Villa Jazzmines, right?” The

pending bubbles were still going and

then they stopped as if the person had

more to say but stopped to give her a

chance to respond. She didn’t respond

instead she contacted Carlos via text:

“The messages are coming again.

From a different number this time. I

thought this was over with. ???? I am

ready to move on. Update me." Sarah

sent the text to Carlos and put her

cellphone on do not disturb. She knew

Ollie would be ready to spend time

together.   Though he was deaf he

certainly could pick up on her energy.

She had to make sure she was all

smiles from inside and out. The more

she heard noise coming from upstairs

indicated to her that Ollie was just

about finished and heading back

downstairs. Sarah's master bedroom

was on the first floor of their home.

They had three bedrooms in their

home. Sarah slept better downstairs.

Occasionally she'd sleep upstairs in

her other master bedroom when Oliver

was having those dreams again. He had one the night before. That's what prompted her to take him to his therapist that morning.   The text messages were coming from an old friend who just couldn't seem to move on. She didn't hate him but she knew it'd be best to move in silence. He didn't feel the same as she.

"Are you ready? I have been waiting

for this moment all my life." Oliver

signed.   Laughing & signing Sarah

responded: "Yes, I am ready. All your

life huh? Me too. I am so glad we

have time to spend together."   Before

Sarah could say another word Oliver

signed asking his mother who was

texting her cellphone. Sarah hesitated

to respond. She forced a smile and

signed back: "No worries. Just an old

friend. They were just checking on

us..me." Oliver picked up on her

changing "us" to "me." Signing he

said: "Are you being honest with me

mommy? I am not just a kid anymore.

It was him wasn't it? Why has your

mood changed? Is something wrong?”

Frozen in her thoughts and hesitation

to respond to him she walked closer to

him as he stood at the foot of their

staircase and reached out to grab his

hand. He grabbed hers. Sarah signed

and said: “Oh, Ollie. I don’t know

what to say or do. Adults don’t always

have the answers, nor do we always

get it right. Yes, that was him texting

me. I feel it's best to just move on and

not look back. Ya, know?" Oliver

hugged his mom then stood back and

signed: "Yes, I understand but you said

to always follow your heart just be

sure to take your mind with you. Are

you doing that this time? What are

you not telling me? Do you think he

has changed?" Sarah suddenly

understood she was no longer

conversing with her little boy but yet a

young man who was applying what

she taught him and using it to guide

her. Signing back Sarah said: "Ollie,

that's the thing. I just don't know. I

have reached out to Carlos. I will let

him handle it. If he has changed and

we are in the clear, then maybe there

can be a tomorrow. The only thing I

know is I will always be with you. I

love…"

Before she could continue her

statement gunshots rang through their

house. One bullet hit Sarah and she

dropped in their kitchen. Oliver didn't

hear anything as he is deaf, but he felt

warmth and pain as soon as his mother

was hit with a bullet to her left temple.

She died instantly. Oliver quickly

remembered what she taught him the

last time they endured this. He bent

down to kiss his mother. He grabbed

her cellphone and ran into her master

bedroom on the first floor where they

were. He remembered there was a

hidden door in her walk-in closet. She

had Carlos and some of his friends

come over to create secret hide-outs

for she and Oliver. He put her

cellphone on mute and locked himself

in the hiding closet. He was too

terrified to tap into his other senses.

He couldn't feel if anyone was inside

the home. His heart was racing, and

he was numb. In shock. He texted

Carlos: "She's been shot, and I don't

think she is alive. A lot of blood and I

am in…" He paused before finishing

his text. He remembered his mother

just told him that she texted Carlos

about the messages coming in again

from "him" yet Carlos hadn't

responded yet. And then all of a

sudden shots were fired into their

home. That was strange. Ollie looked

through the text messages to get any

clues he could to see who all could

have been involved. Being deaf his

other senses were strong and began to

kick in. He placed his hand on the

door to see if he could feel any

vibration. He couldn't at that moment,

but he didn't feel safe enough to make

an exit. Though Carlos was said to be

one of the good guys Ollie was

struggling to consider him one at that moment. Besides, if Carlos was in on what just transpired, he surely didn't want to tell him where he was currently hiding. He didn't feel safe enough to stay inside his home. Let alone a hiding place created by Carlos.

Oliver was stuck.

Pick a side!

"Damn it!!!! I just got the texts. This

damn station has got to do better with

its service.   We have shots fired at

2107 Glenn Mitchell Drive.   No one

has heard a peep out of the tenants.

There is a young woman and one male

child that lives there. I am going to

need back up. It's Sarah for God's

sake! Bake, you're coming with me.

"You got it!" Bake said. Carlos

grabbed his keys off his desk and

proceeded to head to Sarah's house.

Carlos is the lead detective of the Homicide Department at the 3rd Precinct. He was a friend of Sarah's and her current love interest. No one knew about the two of them being intimate as that would have been red flags and a public catastrophe. He worked a case that Sarah and Oliver helped to bring justice to.

Sarah and Oliver's safety was placed

in Carlos' hands. A little while longer

and their relationship would not have

posed suspicion or a threat to anyone.

"Say man. I am really sorry about this.

For you to have received word it must

mean." Bake was saying and got cut

off. "Look, thanks but let's remain

positive at least until we get there. I

mean damn!!!! Anyone could have

gotten hit ya know? Not just her or

Oliver. I can't believe this shit. I have

been waiting to hear back from her on

when this asshole would reach out and

he finally did.   But this dumb ass

service on my cellphone or that jacked

up ass building, and I got nothing until

it was too late. All I needed was time.

DAMN TIME and I didn't get it. Why

the fuck am I being a good person and

trying to do good if bad shit just gone

keep happening."

Carlos was venting. Screaming and then he began to cry. He pulled over and let every emotion out. In front of Bake. A rookie. A newbie. Bake sat inside the squad car and remained silent. He was scared and sad at the same time. He didn't want to say anything and piss Carlos off even more. He didn't want to be silent and seem insensitive. He slowly opened

his car door and got out. He walked

close to Carlos who was standing

behind the squad car weeping. Bake

placed one hand on Carlos' shoulder.

"Say man. Let's get there and see

whats' what. I know this is too much

to handle. But from what I hear you

are the only man for the job. By the

looks of it. We may have survivors at

the address who are now witnesses

or…" Bake said and paused. Carlos

looked up and looked into Bake's eyes.

Carlos' eyes were blood red. He was

numb and afraid.   He didn't know

what he would face, and he really

wasn't ready.   "You right.   DAMN,

this some fucked up shit.   Either way.

Let's go."   Carlos patted Bake on his

shoulder, thanking him for comforting

him during his time of grief and they

got back into the squad car.   While

driving Carlos noticed Bake was doing

a lot of texting. "Ya know not

everything is for everybody? Why you

texting so much? And for the record

shit that happens when you round me

stays round me, ya dig? No lose ships

round here. Got it?" Carlos said. "I

dig. I am just taking notes. Sorry.

Don't mean to make you question me.

Just making sure I keep my emotions

separate from my job. Like you are

doing. That's all. Didn't mean no

harm." Bake said and put his

cellphone away. "You good. I'm

gone be training you. You gone be

learning. We gotta trust one another.

Watch what I do but don't try what I

do. Ya got that? Any questions along

the way. Hold off on them til it's just

me and you around. Ok?" Carlos

said. "I got it. So, if your girlfriend is

the victim here, then what do we do?"

Bake asked. Thrown off Carlos made

a stern face and turned to Bake and

said: "Who said she was my

girlfriend?" Carlos and Bake had

arrived on the scene at Sarah's house.

Bake was afraid to respond.

He swallowed deeply then said: "The

way you cried let me know. My uncle

said a man don't show no emotion

cept' behind his money and woman.

I'm sorry. Just taking notes." Bake

said. "Ya uncle is a smart man. Come

on, Rookie. We got work to do. Stay

close to me. If ya stomach ain't strong

stay out the house. Don't touch

nothing, no pictures, and don't say a

word. You got that? I can't get you

outta something if I don't know what

you get in. Ya dig? Mind ya manners

and don't be everywhere wit

everybody. All folks in uniform don't

mesh well. Ok?" Carlos said. He

didn't take another step forward until

he knew for sure that Bake understood

all that he just said to him and was in

agreement. "OK! Should I stay out of

the kitchen?" Bake said. Carlos

paused as soon as he started stepping

forward. He turned to look at Bake.

Something about him reeked mistrust.

"What did you say your uncle's name

was again?" Carlos asked. "Ummm.

I didn't say." Bake said.

As soon as Carlos was about to say

another word the two men were

greeted by local police officers. "Los.

We have a homicide on our hands. So

far no witnesses and the boy is

missing. No sure if he is still inside

somewhere, ya know? Or if he is just

gone. It's in your hands now. Whose

ya partner here?   Doesn't look

familiar."

Officer Jackson said. "Bake." Carlos

said and turned to face Bake. Carlos

made a face at Bake and it startled

him. Scared Bake said: "Gentlemen."

They both spoke back. Carlos quickly

turned to face the two officers as to not

give away that there was any tension

between, he and Bake.

Though Officer Jackson was going on

and on Carlos was giving him no

indication that he was listening. The

other officer caught on quickly and

interrupted Jackson. "Uhh, let's give

them some breathing room. Holla at

us brother if you need us. We're

heading back to the station for

paperwork." He said and tapped

Office Jackson on his shoulder. As

soon as the two of them were in the

clear and out of Carlos' and Bake's

ears Carlos said: "What the fuck did

you just say? About the kitchen?"

Carlos was standing so close to Bake.

Bake could hear Carlos' heart beating.

"I said did you want me to stay out of

the kitchen?" Bake said. With a smirk

on his face and anger in his eyes

Carlos said: "How did you know of the

location of the victim before we got

here?" With hell in his voice and a

smirk on his face Bake positioned

himself to be extremely close to

Carlos' ear and whispered: "My uncle

always said: "A woman's place is in

the kitchen." Carlos punched Bake in

the face.

Officer Jackson and the other officer

came running back just in time to catch

Bake before he hit the ground. Bake

grabbed his jaw and spit blood out of

his mouth. Officer Jackson grabbed

Carlos and said: "Not here, brother.

Not now. Go inside and do your job.

Let us handle him."

Carlos snatched himself out of Officer

Jackson's grip. "Get him the fuck

outta my face!!! Take him to my

office. I'll yall there soon. Don't let

him out of your sight! I mean that!!!"

Carlos straightened himself up and

continued to give Bake the death stare.

"You got it." Officer Jackson said.

The two officers walked Bake toward

their squad truck and put him in the

back seat. As Carlos was slowly

walking toward Sarah's front door, he

began having flashbacks of their last

conversation about her safety. He had

promised her after this last exchange

they all would be safe and able to live

normal lives again.

No one would be in fear of the

evidence leading back to she or Oliver

helping him capture Luke. Luke was

the man who was texting Sarah earlier.

Though, Bake has been referring to

"his uncle" Carlos wasn't so sure it

was true. Luke wasn't known to have

had any siblings. The puzzle pieces were seeming to be more complex than he bargained for. Just as he was about to open Sarah's front door he got a text from Sarah's cellphone. "I am still here. Are you coming to get me?" It was from Oliver. He was still hiding in the place Carlos had created for him awhile back. Carlos quickly

responded: "Stay quiet. I am here,
buddy. There are so many people
here.

I want to keep you hidden and safe. I
will come to you. Don't make a
sound. Don't move. I'm sorry."

Carlos could see the bubbles form.

Oliver was texting back. "What are
you sorry for?" Carlos couldn't bring

himself to tell him he was sorry for his

loss.   Oliver could see the bubbles

form then they disappeared. Oliver sat

back and waited for Carlos to come

and get him.

Sirens blared, flashing police lights

filled Sarah's street, and neighbors

gathered along her sidewalk waiting to

hear what had taken place in their quiet

middle-to-upper class suburban

community. Their crime rate was low

and the yellow tape was scaring them

so much some of them were looking for their realtors on speed-dial.

The reporters had been camped out on the opposite street as the police were not allowing them to get close and had already threatened them if they even thought about gaining footage or pictures. Carlos was about to step into the unknown and something was tugging at him about Bake. He was

questioning which side was Bake on?

What really happened?

"Boss man. Just the face I was waiting

for." Another detective said to Carlos

as soon as Carlos stepped foot into

Sarah's home. Everything was in slow

motion for Carlos. He could hear the

noise of everyone being around him but the noise seemed muffled. He wanted to run into Sarah's kitchen to see if she was indeed dead there. He knew. His gut told him. But as the lead detective he had to walk his way to the crime scene. He didn't want his emotions to lead him as he needed to remain professional despite. While others were doing their jobs. Securing

the scene, looking for any witnesses,

recording the scene, and searching for

physical evidence, and collecting the

physical evidence his heart was just

about to explode. His heart was

breaking with every minute that

passed. He was trying so hard to keep

his composure and not break down

crying. He didn't want anyone to see
him break.

Every person that came out of the
kitchen to greet him hugged him and
took their hats off. Even though he
knew Sarah was dead he was still in
denial until he saw for himself with his
own two eyes. He maintained his
professionalism and watching

everyone else continue doing their work. He started to either imagine whispers or they were really saying it: "That's his girl." He could have sworn a few officers were saying this out loud. Their facial expressions matched the whispers. He felt like he was losing it. He began to sweat. His pulse was racing. His heartbeat was getting louder every time he'd take a

step closer to the kitchen.

He was getting more pissed. He began

to look at everyone there as a suspect.

He had a few "brothers" in uniform

that knew of his relationship with

Sarah. They were sworn to secrecy.

They could be trusted. Only two of

them were on the scene. They didn't

give it away. They greeted him just

like any other case they'd work

together.

But when out of his presence they both

sent him condolence texts and offered

to meet up later if he needed to talk.

He didn't respond to either text but

when they gave eye contact, he

touched his heart as a way of accepting

their offer. Two more officers to get

through in the living room and Carlos

was to be faced with Sarah. His love.

He was against her using herself in a

previous case against a drug lord. She

was disguised and knew more about

Luke's operation. Luke killed Oliver's

dad some time ago. So as revenge she

felt she'd infiltrate and shut him down

once and for all. For Oliver and her

safety. Luke caught on somehow, well

was tipped off and this is how things

ended. The police and feds were on to

him and one more move from Sarah

would have put him away for life and

shut down his operation. Carlos took a

step toward the kitchen then took a

step back. Bake flashed in his head.

He was trying to pay attention to the

nudge he kept getting and the whisper

form within that was telling him to dig

deeper. His thoughts were asking him

where did Bake come from? How did

he know so much? Who is he? What

side is he really on? How could he get

and keep Oliver safe? So many

thoughts were ringing in his head.

Finally, he stood beside Sarah's

lifeless body. She lay there as if she

were merely sleeping. Carlos got

choked up. He hides his tears well.

One of his officer friends saw him

finally near her and nonchalantly kept

the others from entering into the

kitchen. No one made a fuss of it as

they were trying to put the pieces

together and do their part.

The other officer friend stayed close to

the kitchen entrance as a strong

shoulder to lean on when Carlos

couldn't take seeing her like that

anymore. But all in all they gave him

his space. He kneeled down beside

Sarah and right when his instincts told

him to grab her hand his badge swung

forward and reminded him of his

duties. He couldn't tamper with any

evidence. Letting his emotions touch

her would be tampering and he just

couldn't. He knew he'd get his

moment alone with her. Not then. Not

there.   But soon enough.   Tears

dropped on her body from his eyes and

onto her kitchen floor beside her. At

that moment he felt like he failed her

and Oliver.

The coroners had arrived outside and

would be making their way inside to

gather her remains.

He wasn't ready to let her go just yet.

But he was more than ready to find whoever was responsible for the gut-wrenching pain in his heart that would follow him until whoever was responsible was laying just as Sarah

was.

Lifeless.

Sleep.

Forever!